Summer's
Friendship Games

Autumn's Secret Gift

Winter's Flurry Adventure

Spring's Sparkle Sleepover

Summer's Friendship Games

Summer's Friendship Games

Elise Allen
and Halle Stanford

illustrated by
Paige Pooler

BLOOMSBURY
NEW YORK   LONDON   NEW DELHI   SYDNEY

This book is dedicated to all of the Sparkles and
Weeds who fill our lives every day with their magic:
Max, Theo, Maddie, Wilder, Owen, Jade, Kira,
Charlie, Cate, and Beatrice. And, to Courtney
Bowman, our Summer Sparkle who saved the day.

First published in the United States of America in April 2015
by Bloomsbury Children's Books • www.bloomsbury.com

Bloomsbury is a registered trademark of Bloomsbury Publishing Plc

For information about permission to reproduce selections from this book, write to
Permissions, Bloomsbury Children's Books, 1385 Broadway, New York, NY 10018
Bloomsbury books may be purchased for business or promotional use. For information on
bulk purchases please contact Macmillan Corporate and Premium Sales Department at
specialmarkets@macmillan.com

Library of Congress Cataloging-in-Publication Data
Allen, Elise, author.
Summer's friendship games / by Elise Allen and Halle Stanford ; illustrated by Paige Pooler.
     pages   cm   — (Jim Henson's Enchanted sisters)
Summary: After secretly becoming friends with Thunderbolt, one of the mischievous Weeds,
Summer invites him to her beach party but his brothers tag along, ruining the party, and the
two teams of magical siblings decide to settle their disagreements with a competition, judged
by Mother Nature and Bluster Tempest.
ISBN 978-1-61963-272-1 (paperback) • ISBN 978-1-61963-271-4 (hardcover)
ISBN 978-1-61963-273-8 (e-book)
[1. Seasons—Fiction. 2. Nature—Fiction. 3. Magic—Fiction. 4. Friendship—Fiction.
5. Contests—Fiction. 6. Sisters—Fiction. 7. Brothers—Fiction.] I. Stanford, Halle, author.
II. Pooler, Paige, illustrator. III. Title.
PZ7.A42558Sum 2015   [Fic]—dc23   2014035193

Book design by John Candell
Typeset by Newgen Knowledge Works (P) Ltd., Chennai, India
Printed and bound in the U.S.A. by Thomson-Shore Inc., Dexter, Michigan
2 4 6 8 10 9 7 5 3 1 (paperback)
2 4 6 8 10 9 7 5 3 1 (hardcover)

All papers used by Bloomsbury Publishing, Inc., are natural, recyclable products
made from wood grown in well-managed forests. The manufacturing processes
conform to the environmental regulations of the country of origin.

CHAPTER
1

Shade! Come on! Let's race!"

Summer pushed on her jaguar friend's thick, furry side. She itched to stretch her legs and sprint across the new trail she and Shade had discovered in her Sparkledom beyond the Rainbow River.

Shade opened her green eyes and yawned, showing off a mouth of impossibly sharp teeth before falling back asleep.

"Are you kidding me?" Summer cried. "You're a fierce jungle jaguar! Show some competitive spirit!"

Summer and Shade had taken a little siesta under their favorite Brazilian pepper tree after a morning romp of vine swinging and branch jumping in the Resplendent Rainforest. Now that she was up, Summer didn't want to waste another moment of

sunshine. She turned her back to Shade, dug into the ground with her feet, and leaned against the jaguar's flank with all her might. "C'mo-o-o-n, ya bi-i-g kiiiiitty!" But she couldn't move her.

"You're hopeless," she said affectionately. The jaguar's whiskers twitched before she rolled over to bake in the sun.

"Okay, Sleepy!" she told Shade. "Take your cat-nap, but make sure to meet me in an hour at Sparkle Shores. I need help setting up for my Summer Blast-off Beach Party tonight!"

Summer felt as buzzy as a hummingbird. Every year, in the middle of her season, she hosted a beach party for her sisters that celebrated everything fun and sunny in her Sparkledom!

Summer loved planning ways for her sisters to get together, relax, and play. The four sisters were

Seasonal Sparkles, charged with changing the seasons in the Outworld. It was a big job but, thanks to the joining of their Sparkle Powers, scepters, headbands, and the help of Mother Nature, they were always able to keep nature in balance. They all took their duties seriously, so Summer felt it was *her* duty to remind them to also have FUN! She needed to be the one to prompt Autumn to be silly, or urge Spring to focus all of her bubbly energy, or—most important—challenge Winter to a new game.

Looking up at the sun, Summer realized she still had time before she really needed to race over to Sparkle Shores and string up the paper lanterns, set up the beach torches, and decorate the picnic tables. She reached to the small of her back and pulled her scepter from its holster. The orb was still bright yellow. When it was time for her and her sisters to perform the Sparkle Ceremony and turn summer to autumn for the Outworlders, the orb would turn silver. The sisters had never been to the Outworlders' realm, but Mother Nature had told them stories. Most of the Outworlders spent the summer taking vacations, relaxing, and enjoying the outdoors—all the things Summer relished. Mother Nature said schoolchildren especially looked forward to summer all year long, and Summer had beamed with pride, knowing her season was their favorite.

Summer put her scepter back into its holster and turned around to view her Sparkledom. Every Sparkle had her own Sparkledom that perfectly reflected each sister's season and personality. Summer's was a mirror of her sunny spirit. As always, it was beautiful and had all her favorite things: huge fields of brown-tipped grass; shimmering ponds and Rainbow River for swimming, boating, and waterskiing; and a forest filled with paths promising adventure and shady trees. Towering above the canopy of the Resplendent Rainforest, her multitiered wooden lodge nestled between two giant ceiba trees crowned with ever-blossoming hot-pink flowers. Hanging from the lodge and tree branches were vine ladders, hammocks, and climbing nets. A colorful tunnel slide and a spiral staircase encircled one of the green trunks. Both ran up to the tip of a crow's nest that overlooked all of Summer's Sparkledom.

"CAW!"

Summer looked up. A red-and-yellow macaw peered down at her from a palm tree. She didn't have Spring's power to talk to animals, but by the way the macaw looked at Shade and then turned back to Summer with his head cocked, she could tell he was saying, "That gal won't do you any good. Try me!"

Grinning, she stood and kicked off her shoes so she could feel the ground beneath her feet.

"You're on," she said. "To Rainbow River. Ready. Set. GO!"

Summer sprinted down the hill as the macaw took off from the branch. He flew low, teasing her with his black tail feathers just in front of her head. Summer ran faster, leaning into the steep descent, her long brown hair whipping around her. She didn't even look down, leaping nimbly over each obstacle.

Pouring on the speed, Summer twisted past thick tree trunks and darted under sinewy branches until she couldn't see the bird at all—not even a flash of red. She allowed herself a quick glance back to check the size of her lead, and . . .

CRACK!

Summer whipped her head around just in time to see the branch collapse in front of her. She was running too fast to stop! She slammed into it and tumbled over, landing flat on her back.

"OW!"

She immediately rolled over and reached for her scepter, studying the orb. Unbroken. Thank goodness. She would hate to ask Mother to fix her mess. The scepter was Summer's responsibility and it was vital for her to do her job one hundred percent!

Suddenly, Summer heard cackling laughter just like the whining hum of electricity above her head. She sprang to her feet. "Thunderbolt!"

Thunderbolt was one of the Weeds, rowdy boys who could magically control natural disasters. They were the Sparkles' worst enemies and worked for the dreaded Bluster Tempest. Bluster and the Weeds lived to cause chaos and stop the seasons from changing. Thunderbolt was rolling around on a low black storm cloud, giggling so hard he couldn't even sit upright. His ratty pants and jacket blended in with the cloud so well that if it weren't for his purple spiked hair and the lightning bolt on his T-shirt, Summer would never have been able to spot him.

"Stop it!" Summer snapped. "That wasn't funny!"

"Sure it was," Thunderbolt snorted. "You should have seen the look on your face." He sat up and widened his eyes in panic, pinwheeling his arms. "Whoooooaaaa!!!!"

He collapsed backward onto the cloud, chortling.

Summer glared at him, her hands on her hips. She clenched her jaw, concentrated her powers, and chanted:

> "Frizzle, frazzle, fry, and snuff!
> Sizzle his cloud to go up in a puff!"

A beam of pure heat energy shot out of her scepter and into Thunderbolt's storm cloud, evaporating it at once. Thunderbolt stopped laughing, his face falling as he thumped to the ground.

"OW!"

With a flip of her hair, Summer turned and marched away from Thunderbolt. Was there anything in the world more annoying than the Weeds?

* * **7** * *

"That's it?" Thunderbolt called after her. "You're just gonna walk away and not say you're sorry?"

Summer gasped and wheeled to face him. He had pulled himself off the ground and was rubbing his rear end. His mouth was twisted in a sulky frown.

"*Me,* say I'm sorry?" Summer cried. "You came to *my* Sparkledom and ruined my race! What else did you plan to do? Steal my scepter?!"

"Aw, come on," Thunderbolt said. "Just admit it. You're a little sore because you weren't gonna outrun the macaw. You're not that fast."

"Bet I'm faster than you."

"Bet you're not."

"Race you to the giant boulder." Summer pointed to a rock beside the river. It was only about fifty yards away—the perfect distance to measure speed.

"You're closer. That's cheating."

Summer rolled her eyes. She was only a few feet closer to the boulder than Thunderbolt. She dug her toe into the ground, drawing a straight line.

"We'll start here," she said. "Same distance."

Thunderbolt trudged over, still rubbing his bruised bottom. Summer's lips twitched—she fell way harder than he did, and she wasn't moping around. "You count it off," she said.

"Okay. One . . . *two-three-go!*"

He sprinted off, grabbing a head start, the pain in his rear end apparently gone.

Leave it to a Weed to cheat.

Summer leaped into action, sprinting harder than she thought she could. Everything else faded away; she concentrated on closing in on the single jagged violet streak in Thunderbolt's hair . . .

"Ha-ha," Thunderbolt sang a few feet from the boulder. "You lo—"

Summer lunged ahead and smacked the boulder before him.

"I lo—ve to win?" she offered.

They were so close her hair whipped his face as she turned around. Thunderbolt wiped his face, looking genuinely confused.

"How did you . . . ? What did you . . . ?" Thunderbolt spluttered.

"What did I what?" Summer teased. She pointed her finger at his chest. "I beat you!" She laughed and Thunderbolt flashed a crooked grin.

"Rematch!" he shouted playfully.

"No way!" she said coolly, pulling her hair behind her ears. "I won. Fair and square. Admit it—I'm faster than you."

But Thunderbolt wasn't looking at Summer anymore. His gaze had drifted up and his jaw dropped. Summer put her hand to her head.

Her headband was gone. It had fallen off during the race.

Summer gasped. She and Thunderbolt zoomed back across the grass, retracing their steps. Summer kept her eyes on the ground. The band was the same leafy green as her eyes, dress, and scepter, and she knew it could blend in with the deep grass. She was counting on Thunderbolt to miss it.

Then she heard him scream, "YES!"

Summer felt her heart drop. The headband had rolled under a log; next to the dark brown of the bark, its green practically shouted its location. Thunderbolt was going to get it and take it away, and it was all Summer's fault.

CHAPTER
2

NOOOO!" Summer roared. As she bounded forward at full speed, she hoisted her scepter and drove it into a hump in the ground ahead of her. Although it was only a little longer than the length of her arm, she was still able to use the momentum to vault herself into the air feetfirst, toward Thunderbolt.

"Look out!" she warned him.

Thunderbolt glanced over his shoulder. His mouth and eyes swelled to giant Os, and he was too surprised to even move . . . until Summer's feet smacked into his chest and knocked him down. Summer thudded to the ground right next to him and grabbed the headband. She stood up and placed it back on her head, smoothing her wild hair beneath it.

"Sorry I kicked you," Summer told Thunderbolt. "I tried to warn you so you could get out of the way. I just couldn't let you get the headband."

"Yeah, thanks," Thunderbolt said, rubbing his chest. "I was just trying to help. I didn't want your stupid head—hey! Did you really just vault over that thing?"

The second he said "that thing," Summer wanted to smack herself. Her scepter, just as precious as her headband, was still lodged in the ground. They both looked at it, and Summer prepared to race off again . . . when Thunderbolt bowed his head and extended his arms toward it. "Your scepter, milady."

Was this some kind of trick?

Summer kept her eyes on him as she walked to the scepter, yanked it out of the dirt, and tucked it back into its holster. Thunderbolt had a weird look on his face.

"What?" she asked.

"Nothing. I just thought, maybe . . . you think you could teach me to do that? That vaulting thing?" he added, dropping his eyes and studying his scuffed shoe.

He raised his beady black eyes to meet Summer's and smiled. A genuine smile, not his usual sneer.

Summer scrunched her eyebrows. She considered asking what Bluster would do if he found out one of his Weeds was being nice to a Sparkle, but she already knew the answer. He'd be furious. Thunderbolt had to know it too, but if he was still willing to be nice, why mess it up by reminding him?

Summer returned his smile. "Okay," she said. "I'll teach you. But what are you going to do for me? Can you teach me how to make lightning?"

Thunderbolt scratched the back of his purple spiked hair. "I can't. I don't even know how *I* make lightning. I just use this stick here to help me channel it." Thunderbolt reached into his dirty sock, pulled out his stick, and casually flicked his wrist. The sky CRACKED and a bolt of lightning struck the ground two feet from Summer.

"Whoops," said Thunderbolt.

Summer gave him her best reproachful glare. "So, lightning's out . . ." There was something Summer wanted to ask, but it was a little embarrassing.

"The last time I saw you in the Barrens, you were diving into a pool from the top of your thunder-cloud," she began.

"Oh, yeah," Thunderbolt sneered. "You and Winter wrapped us up in mud and froze us together for hours."

Summer stifled a giggle. "Anyway," she continued, "do you think you could teach me to dive into the Rainbow River from the top of your thundercloud?"

Thunderbolt snorted. "You don't know how to high-dive into a pool?"

Summer felt her cheeks go red and turned away. "Forget I said anything. Maybe you should just go home."

She started walking back to where Shade was sleeping, but Thunderbolt grabbed her arm. She wheeled around and he dropped his hand like her arm was on fire.

"Sorry," he said. "I didn't mean . . . I just thought, you know, that you'd be really good at it."

Summer considered sending him home anyway, but he seemed sincere, and maybe he could help.

"I get *how* to dive. I just . . ." She lowered her voice. "I've never jumped from high up before. It always seemed a little too scary to me."

"You're just scared 'cause you haven't been up there a lot. I'll help you. You'll like it."

He sounded so sure about it, like it wasn't a big deal at all that she was afraid. "You think so?" she asked.

"Oh, yeah! And you'll show me the vault thing, right?"

"Yeah, definitely! It's easy—you'll get it right away."

"Great! So . . . deal."

"Deal."

When their hands touched, they created a hot white spark. Summer and Thunderbolt yelped and burst out laughing.

"What a shockingly good deal!" Thunderbolt said. He pointed his stick at the ground and shouted, "*Clooouuuddeerrrvaaattor!*"

A small thundercloud formed at their feet. Thunderbolt confidently hopped onto the cloud. Summer followed with a front handspring.

"*Girls,*" Thunderbolt groaned.

Summer smiled as the thundercloud lifted into the air and headed toward Rainbow River. Soaring on a thundercloud was almost like riding a surfboard in slow motion, except the cloud undulated beneath her instead of waves. This was A BLAST!

The thundercloud settled above the part of Rainbow River that rushed in a huge waterfall from Spring's Sparkledom into Summer's realm. The river flowed through all of the Sparkledoms, earning its name. But Summer thought it also deserved to be called Rainbow River because the surface of the water shimmered with a million rainbow prisms.

"This looks like a good spot to learn," Thunderbolt proclaimed.

Summer felt her mouth go dry.

"Listen, Sparkle, it's a long way down, so ya gotta go feetfirst. Once, Quake went down a dive headfirst and his head was ringing for days."

"I don't think it ever stopped ringing," Summer said.

Thunderbolt snickered before growing serious again. "All you have to do is imitate the waterfall and keep your eye on it," he advised, pointing at the rush of the water. "It's a straight shot down. I'll go first and show you."

It might be weird, but Summer thought he genuinely wanted to teach her.

Like a friend.

"Okay, start with your arms above your head like this," Thunderbolt instructed. He held his arms over his head with his hands creating a point. "Then, take a deep breath and spit." He spit over the edge of the thundercloud.

Ewww, thought Summer.

"And then . . . follow the waterfall!" he shouted, and jumped off of the thundercloud, facing the waterfall. Summer's stomach dropped. When Thunderbolt hit the river, his body disappeared under the shimmer of rainbows. Summer held her breath until he resurfaced and shouted, "WOO-HOO!"

Summer smiled and gave Thunderbolt a thumbs-up. He pointed up at her and shouted, "Your turn, Summer!"

Summer closed her eyes and took a deep breath. The sound of the surging waterfall in front of her was surprisingly soothing. She opened her eyes and spit over the thundercloud.

Then she looked down.

It was a very long way.

Thunderbolt shouted, "Nice spit!"

"Thunderbolt?" she cried, her voice quavering. She wasn't sure she could actually jump. The height, the roar of the waterfall, and her shaking knees started to overwhelm her.

Thunderbolt swam so he was right under the thundercloud and called up, "You got this, Summer!

Just pretend your body is the waterfall! You'll be down here so fast you won't even be able to escape from my super splashing." He splashed some water up in her direction.

Summer didn't want to back down. But she wasn't sure she could do it. If Winter were here, she would already be gloating at Summer's hesitation. Autumn would tell her she could try when she was ready. Spring would encourage her to come and float down Rainbow River on one of her flower-shaped inner tubes.

Thunderbolt's voice cut through her fear . . . like lightning. "You can do it, Summer! Be the waterfall. Be the waterfall!"

And with that, Summer jumped feetfirst off the edge of the thundercloud.

As she plunged down toward the river, she imagined herself falling as lightly and swiftly as the waterfall. Her skirt flew up and she was relieved that she was wearing her green leggings underneath. At last, her pointed toes pierced through the rainbow prisms and her body plummeted into the cool water.

I did it! she thought, relieved and exhilarated. She couldn't wait to hear what Thunderbolt thought of her dive!

As she broke the surface of Rainbow River, she was immediately splashed in the face with a wave of water.

"I told you to get ready for a super splashing!" Thunderbolt teased.

"Oh, you rotten Weed! No fair!" Summer laughed, quickly ducking beneath the water. She yanked on Thunderbolt's legs and pulled him below the surface. When he bobbed up for breath, she spit a mouthful of water in his face.

"Ack!" yelled Thunderbolt, wiping his face. "You tricky Sparkle!" He swam away, kicking giant splashes of water.

"Hey, Thunderbolt!" Summer shouted.

The Weed stopped swimming when he was out of splashing range. "What?"

"Thanks," Summer said, smiling. "That high dive was really fun. And you were right about keeping my eyes on the waterfall. Good advice."

Thunderbolt shyly looked down at the water. "No one's ever told me I give good advice. Actually, nobody has ever told me I do anything well."

Summer wasn't sure what to say. It must be terrible never to be told you do anything well. She suddenly felt sorry for Thunderbolt and wondered if he ever had a real friend.

"Hey," Thunderbolt said with a crooked smile. "Do you want to learn how to dive with a somersault this time?"

"Would I ever!" Summer answered, ready for the next lesson from her new unlikely friend.

CHAPTER
3

Summer ran in her green bikini toward the magnif-icent sand castles, carrying two buckets of seawater. Creating wild sand art with her sisters was one of her favorite things to do at her Blastoff Beach Party. The Sparkles had decided this year to create sand castles that looked like each of their homes.

"Do you need any help?" Autumn asked. Sum-mer's sister was resting in her adorable orange-and-yellow-striped one-piece on a rainbow beach blanket, her loose black hair covered by a giant red sun hat. She had already whipped up a perfect replica of her exotic palace, complete with a mini sand version of her elephant friend, Whisper.

"No, thanks!" Summer answered, realizing she had lost half a pail of water along the way. "We're

almost done. Next is dinner. I've made your favorite seaweed salad!"

Autumn murmured, "Mmmmm." She put on her sunglasses and sipped her tropical smoothie through a red striped straw.

Summer's Lodge was already sculpted. Right now it was Winter's Sand Sparkledom that they really needed to finish.

"Two buckets . . . at your service!" Summer declared, setting the buckets next to Winter.

"Cool!" said Winter, grabbing one of the buckets and pouring its water into a brick-shaped plastic mold. They had already finished Winter's Chalet, but then they decided to build a sand version of her ice igloo fort too. Summer wasn't sure they could finish before the sun set. She also noticed that Winter's legs, arms, hair in pigtails, and white skirted bathing suit with sequined snowflakes were covered in pink sand. They might need to use one of the buckets to clean Winter up before dinner. After all, she knew Winter always liked to look her best—and tonight they might have a surprise guest.

Summer had invited Thunderbolt to her Blastoff Beach Bonfire. They'd had so much fun high-diving earlier that they'd run out of time for her to teach him how to pole-vault, and so she had impulsively invited him to the party. He said he'd think about it—and she still owed him a vaulting lesson—but if he did come, it would be when the bonfire actually started. She hadn't told her sisters, yet. She just hoped they wouldn't be angry with her and that Thunderbolt would mind his manners.

Summer carefully helped Winter lift the brick mold onto the top of the igloo wall. They turned it over and out plunked another wet sand brick. "Only two dozen more to go!" said Summer with a smile. "Hey, where's Spring?"

"She decided to build a shell garden for her sand castle," Winter said, pointing her thumb farther down the beach.

Summer could see Spring skipping over the water in her swim cap and bikini made of purple and pink fabric flowers. She had a giant green inner tube around her tummy and leaned down every now and then to pick up a shell and plop it in her pink bucket.

Summer imagined Spring also wanted to sneak away and chat with the sea life. She always said sea creatures had the funniest stories to share.

"We need more water to make more bricks," Winter declared, grabbing the buckets and sprinting off. Now was the perfect time for Summer to break away and set up their feast.

She had to admit the party food on the picnic tables looked scrumptious. There were colorful buckets filled with fish crackers and pretzels shaped like octopi, platters of skewered grilled vegetables, a tangy seaweed salad, and a watermelon basket filled with fruit cut out like sea stars. There was still plenty of the tropical smoothie left, as well as pitchers of ice water with seashell-shaped ice cubes (courtesy of Winter). Summer set the table with surfboard-shaped plates and utensils fashioned like different sea animals. She wanted everything to be perfectly beachy for her sisters!

She pointed her scepter and chanted:

"Light the flames around this beach,
Make everything glow within my reach!"

Yellow sparkles flew out of Summer's scepter and danced around the beach like fireflies. One by one, each spark ignited a flame that lit up the torches, lanterns, and candles. As the sun started to set, the little orange lights all around the party mirrored its brilliance. Blastoff Beach Party perfection.

Summer put her fingers in her mouth and whistled loudly. "C'mon, Sparkles!" she shouted. "Dinnertime!"

As her sisters joined her at the table, Summer once again wondered how best to bring up the subject of Thunderbolt.

"Working on a sand igloo can sure make a girl hungry!" Winter exclaimed, shoveling fish crackers onto her plate.

"Cockles and mussels!" Spring said, nibbling on another piece of watermelon shaped like a crab. "I know what you mean. It took me ten tries before I found a conch shell that actually didn't have a conch living in it. Snails are very fussy about leaving their homes." She lifted the shell to her lips and blew a loud honk.

All the Sparkles covered their ears as the conch shell trumpeted around the beach. Winter shouted, "Spring! *I'm* very fussy about keeping my hearing."

"Oops," Spring said, with an apologetic smile. "Sorry, Winter. I've just got a lot of wind in me."

Winter laughed so hard that fish crackers fell out of her mouth. "Spring, you have to quit saying everybody has a lot of wind. It means something else entirely."

Spring scrunched up her face, trying to figure out what her sister meant.

"Oh!" she finally cried, her eyes popping open. "You are as bad as the Weeds!"

Summer, Winter, and Autumn couldn't help but giggle. In playful retaliation, Spring stood on top of the picnic table and blew the conch as loud as she could. She finished her trumpeting with a final splutter that sounded like a large animal passing gas.

"*Now* who's the Weed?" Autumn teased Spring.

Spring chuckled and jumped down into the sand. "I may be windy, but I'm way too delightful to be a Weed."

"Don't forget clean," Winter added.

Summer was starting to regret inviting Thunderbolt. What was she going to do? He could arrive at any moment. "I'm sure the Weeds have some good qualities," she said hesitantly.

"Yeah, staying put in the Barrens where they belong," Winter said, stabbing her grilled vegetables with a skewer.

"About that . . . ," Summer said, offering a platter of cookies decorated like flip-flops to her sisters.

"Yum!" Winter said. "What's next on the Blastoff Beach Party agenda?"

"I was thinking we could have a water balloon toss," said Summer, wishing she knew how to tell her sisters the truth.

"Water balloon toss sounds great!" Winter exclaimed.

Summer grabbed the giant red bucket of water balloons that she had filled up earlier, dragging them out into an open patch of sand away from the tables. Maybe Thunderbolt wouldn't come. Why would he want to hang out with a bunch of Sparkles playing with water balloons and roasting marshmallows around a bonfire? He would probably rather wrestle with his smelly brothers, throw rocks at rotting logs, and swim in a stinky marsh. They did have a blast high-jumping off of his thundercloud earlier, though. She still couldn't believe she had mustered the courage to try a somersault jump. Thunderbolt had called it the Summer Somersault.

"C'mon, Autumn," Summer shouted. "You're my partner for the balloon toss!"

The four Sparkles grabbed armfuls of water balloons and took their positions.

The point of the game was to see which team could get the farthest away and still catch the water balloon without it breaking. Summer wished that Autumn had better aim so she didn't have to keep running in all directions to catch her sister's tosses.

"Spring!" Winter shouted. "You're doing great! Have you been practicing?"

"No," Spring replied. "I'm just imagining I'm catching a baby robin's egg that's fallen from its nest."

Summer hated to think what would happen if Spring dropped a balloon. They would probably have to spend an hour assuring her that she wouldn't *really* drop a robin's egg.

"Rain!" Autumn shouted, pointing to the sky behind Summer's head.

Summer turned around and saw a small black thundercloud racing toward Sparkle Shores. *Oh, no.* Her tummy rumbled like the lightning surrounding the cloud.

"That's not rain!" Winter screamed. "It's the Weeds!"

As the thundercloud loomed above them, Summer could see Thunderbolt and his brothers, Twister, Quake, and Sleet, standing next to him. They were all shirtless and dressed for the beach in cutoff pants and ragged shorts. Why had he invited his brothers? This was a disaster.

All of her Sparkle Sisters took action. Winter and Autumn aimed their scepters at the thundercloud hovering overhead. Spring squealed and ran toward their sand castles, taking refuge inside the sand igloo. Summer needed to tell them what was happening.

"Wait!" she shouted. "Let me explain!"

Autumn started to chant:

"Summer winds hear my plea,
Blow this thundercloud back out to—"

Before she could finish, Thunderbolt flew their thundercloud down to the sandy surface and the Weeds dismounted in full water-gun attack mode. "Charge!" Thunderbolt shouted, hitting Autumn in the face with his soaker.

"Stop!" Summer yelled. "Thunderbolt! What are you doing?"

Thunderbolt didn't answer as he and Sleet launched into a water-balloon-versus-water-soaker war with Winter. Autumn hurled water balloons at Twister while he deflected them with a mini tornado. Quake, who wore an old-fashioned black bathing suit, lumbered over to where Spring was hiding in the sand igloo. He jumped up and down, and his heavy body caused an earthquake that demolished all of the sand art. Spring escaped the fallen igloo and raced back to her sisters.

Summer decided to help Winter, furious that Thunderbolt would come to her party and try to ruin it. She jumped in front of Winter and faced Thunderbolt squarely.

"What are you doing?" she asked, her hands on her hips.

He smiled and said, "I told you I was a super splasher, Sparkle!" Then he sprayed her with his soaker, dousing her face, hair, and neon-green bikini. She felt water balloons hitting her arms, and a steady stream of water hitting her back. She was being attacked from all sides!

"ENOUGH!" she shouted, holding her scepter up in the air. "One more squirt and I'll dry up all the water in every single soaker, balloon, and water gun!"

Everything went still. Summer opened her eyes to see all the Weeds and Sparkles staring at one another menacingly.

"How dare you come and crash our party!" Winter exclaimed, pointing her scepter at Thunderbolt.

"Crash your party?" Thunderbolt asked, confused. "Summer invited me."

Everybody turned to look at Summer, standing there dripping from head to toe. She wished she could disappear just like the sun had beyond the horizon.

CHAPTER
4

"**S**ummer would never spoil her Blastoff Beach Party by inviting you Weeds," Autumn proclaimed.

"Summer wouldn't invite the Weed who broke my scepter," Spring huffed, glaring at Thunderbolt.

"Or a Weed that tried to steal my polar bear, Flurry!" Winter fumed, moving in between Thunderbolt and Summer.

Summer felt sick. Her sisters were right. Thunderbolt had been awful in the past. But he was so kind earlier she had just forgotten. "I should have told you girls before," she said, trying to keep her voice calm. "But I did invite Thunderbolt to the party tonight. I just didn't know he'd invite the other Weeds!"

"He didn't invite us!" Twister wheezed.

"They jumped on my thundercloud at the last second," Thunderbolt explained, sounding a teeny bit apologetic. "I didn't think it would be a big deal if they came along."

Summer felt less annoyed with Thunderbolt. "Well . . . ," she started.

"You invited Thunderbolt to our Blastoff Beach Party?!" Winter shouted, squeezing a water balloon.

"You see, earlier when I was racing this macaw, I . . . ," Summer spluttered nervously. Winter had never been so upset with her. It made her feel hot and confused.

"She invited me because I taught her to high-dive," Thunderbolt said proudly.

"You did what?" Twister and Sleet said together.

"Yeah, in Rainbow River," Thunderbolt said, smiling.

"You never taught *me* to high-dive," Quake grumbled, kicking up the sand.

"That's because you're too busy clipping your toe-nails and picking them with your teeth!" Thunderbolt teased, and pushed Quake down into the sand.

"Ewww!" said Autumn and Spring.

Winter got up in Summer's face. "He taught you to high-dive? In Rainbow River?" she asked, shaking her head in disbelief. "I could have taught you to do that."

"She even did the Summer Somersault!" Thunderbolt bragged.

Summer felt trapped by her sisters and annoyed with the Weeds. "We *did* go high-diving today," Summer confessed. She looked over at Thunderbolt. "And . . . it was fun." She smiled. Thunderbolt's face softened.

"Well," said Autumn, taking a step toward her, "if you did invite him, then we should go back to the party. But we should all watch our scepters." Autumn gave Summer a hesitant smile and walked over to the picnic table.

"I'm going to go and fix our sand Sparkledoms," declared Spring. She marched off toward the demolished sand art, clutching her scepter.

Summer felt relieved that her sisters understood. Then Winter icily stomped by her, calling out to Spring,

"I'll help you, Spring." Summer would need to speak with her sister in private.

"So what now, Sparkle?" Thunderbolt asked, pulling Summer's attention away from Winter.

"Well," Summer said, indicating the picnic table, "there's a lot of yummy food you could eat. I made flip-flop cookies. But no eating them with your feet, okay?"

"YUM!" Quake shouted, waddling over to the picnic table.

"We were also building sand art," Summer said, pointing to where Spring and Winter were repairing the sand igloo fort.

"Sleet," Thunderbolt said, tapping his brother on the shoulder. "You like making stuff out of slush and mud. Maybe you could go and help them fix their little castles." He thrust his thumb toward Winter and Spring.

"C'mon, icicle face," Twister barked. "Let's go. I have a hilarious idea . . ." Sleet and Twister walked over to Winter and Spring, whispering and wheezing.

Summer felt a little shy when she turned back to face Thunderbolt. "Let's gather the wood for the bonfire," she suggested.

"I'll get the wood and you find some tinder!" Thunderbolt said excitedly. He dashed along the beach, gathering up branches of driftwood.

Summer collected a pile of dried seaweed for the tinder and Thunderbolt dropped a pile of wood where she indicated she wanted the bonfire.

"Now watch as I build a master bonfire," Thunderbolt said, cracking his knuckles. "Watch this!"

He pointed his crooked stick at the pile of wood and seaweed and shouted, "*Flmmrrrzzzkkllle!*" A bolt of white lightning shot from Thunderbolt's stick and ignited the bonfire.

"Now what do we do?" he asked. "Jump over it?"

"No." Summer laughed. "We roast marshmallows over it."

"I guess that's the second-best thing you could do with a bonfire," Thunderbolt said.

"Definitely." Summer smiled.

Soon the only light on the beach was from the roaring bonfire and the stars twinkling above. The Sparkles stayed on one side of the bonfire and the Weeds on the other. Winter and Spring were

still sore over Twister and Sleet building sand sharks and giant squids attacking their sand castles.

"How do the marshmallows taste?" Summer asked, desperate for anyone to talk.

"I've got a song!" Twister shouted, and he began singing in a high piggy voice:

"Now what's the good of being a Weed?
Farting and spitting, that's our creed!
Some say we stink and our soap is charcoal,
But . . . better to be a Weed . . .
Than a silly Sparkle!
Sparkles, Sparkles,
Silly, silly girls!

All fluff and fuss
With rainbows and curls!"

The other Weeds started clapping and stomping along with Twister. Quake even got up and started dancing, his belly jiggling. The brothers all joined in loudly for the last chorus, then fell back on the sand, snorting and hooting:

"Now what's the good of being a Weed?
Farting and spitting, that's our creed!
Some say we stink and our soap is charcoal,
But . . . better to be a Weed . . .
Than a silly Sparkle!"

Summer was angry and embarrassed. "That was a terrible song," she said sternly. Thunderbolt tried to stifle his laughter, but the Weeds kept crowing.

"So, you think a Weed is better than a Sparkle?" Winter asked, standing up.

"At practically everything," Sleet answered, also standing up.

"Think you could beat me in a toboggan race down the Sugar Slopes?"

"With my eyes closed and my pants over my head." Sleet laughed.

"Think you could run through the mud, muck, lava, and thicket of the Barrens?" Twister dared.

"Faster than you," Autumn said.

"I dare you to a race in my Sparkledom!" Winter cried. "Sparkles against the Weeds."

"Then I dare you to a race in the Barrens!" Sleet hissed.

"Done," Winter agreed, stomping her foot in the sand.

"You won't even finish the race," Thunderbolt said. "Well, maybe Summer would, but none of the rest of you Sparkles have a chance."

Summer blushed. Nobody had ever said that she was better than her sisters at anything. Nevertheless, this bonfire was starting to feel like an out-of-control wildfire. "I'm not sure this is a great idea."

"You're right," Thunderbolt said.

Summer sighed with relief.

"A *great* idea," Thunderbolt declared, holding his finger in the air for emphasis, "would be to hold a race in *every* Sparkledom *and* the Barrens!"

"And what will be the prize for the winners?" Autumn said.

"We should let Mother Nature decide," Spring answered excitedly.

"And Bluster!" Quake added.

"Fine," Winter said. "The first challenge will be in my realm tomorrow. Toboggan race. We'll invite Mother Nature and Bluster Tempest to declare the winner."

"C'mon, Weeds!" hollered Thunderbolt. "Let's get going so we can get ready to waste some Sparkles in the snow tomorrow." He pointed his stick at the ground and barked, "*Clooouuuddeerrrvaaattor!*"

Steaming out of Thunderbolt's stick, another large thundercloud formed along the sand. The Weeds grabbed their soakers, squirt guns, and the bag of marshmallows, and clambered on board their stormy transportation home. As the cloud lifted away, Thunderbolt yelled down, "Thanks for the bonfire,

Summer! Even though I built it!" Then the Weeds flew away, faster than a hurricane.

Summer gave Thunderbolt a small smile, but she was afraid to wave with her sisters staring at her.

"Yes, thank you for the Blastoff Beach Party, Summer," Autumn said, gathering up her hat and bag. "The seaweed salad was stupendous. But I think it's time for us to leave now too."

"I didn't mean for this to happen," Summer apologized.

"We know," Winter said, squeezing her hand. "Thunderbolt tricked you."

Summer wasn't sure that Thunderbolt *had* tricked her. But she didn't want to argue with Winter. Not now.

"See ya later, Summer," Winter said. "Meet us on top of the Sugar Slopes early tomorrow morning. We'll show those Weeds who's gonna waste whom!"

Summer couldn't believe her sisters were leaving.

Winter, Autumn, and Spring lifted their scepters high up in the air and chanted:

"Rainbow, rainbow, reunite,
Fly on colored wings of light!
Away to our homes all safe and sound
until our feet touch the ground."

Rainbow light shone from the gems on each Sparkle's headband, joining together to make one colorful pathway to the sky. One by one, the Sparkles leaped into the magical light of the rainbow that would take each of them back to their Sparkledoms. All three girls waved at Summer, shouting, "Thanks" and "See you tomorrow!"

Summer waved back at her sisters until the sparkling rainbow arch disappeared along with their tiny figures, then turned to stare sadly at the gentle waves of the sea. All she had wanted was for her sisters and new friend to get along. Instead, her gesture of friendship to Thunderbolt had turned into an unfriendly challenge between her sisters and the Weeds. Maybe Sparkles and Weeds weren't meant to be friends after all.

CHAPTER
5

The early morning sunlight shimmered on Sugar Slopes, and the snow on the mountain peaks swirled around Summer like butter frosting on a cupcake. As she reached the top where her sisters were waiting, a ball of fur sprang into the air—it was Winter, doing jump squats in her parka.

"Come on!" she called, spying Summer. "Get those hamstrings ready to race!"

Immediately, the ground began to rumble. From a gaping hole above them dropped the Weeds and a gnarly black toboggan: Sleet first, zooming in on a shard of ice, then Quake behind him, and finally Twister and Thunderbolt on a dark, gloomy cloud. Thunderbolt winked at Summer as he landed. Summer shot him a small smile, then turned back as the sky cracked and Bluster Tempest dropped down. He looked like a hulking skunk in his tuxedo, one size too small for his rotund belly. Summer took a step back. She didn't mind him so much when Mother Nature was around, but when he was alone, he made her want to hide behind the nearest snowbank and wait for him to leave.

"Salivations and salutations," Bluster bellowed, rolling out his top hat in a ceremonial bow. "How are the lovely Sparkle girls this fine morning?"

"Ready to lose?" a grinning Sleet asked, his eyebrows pointing down his nose mischievously.

"Not to a lousy Weed!" Winter said hotly.

"Winter," said a warning voice. "I thought this was a friendly event." They turned. Mother Nature was standing behind them, her elegant turtledove advisor, Serenity, perched lightly on her soft, creamy shawl. She wore a stylish turquoise tunic, fleece leggings, and shaggy white boots that looked as warm as Flurry the polar bear.

"Mother Nature!" Spring cried, and hopped up like a sparrow to bury her face in Mother's shawl.

"We're about to toboggan-race against the Weeds, and we're going to race against them in the other Sparkledoms and the Barrens too, to prove to them that Sparkles are definitely better than rotten Weeds!"

Mother Nature's brows tensed. For a moment, Summer could have sworn she saw her frown. "Surely my girls know better than that," she said. "Girls are not better than boys. And Sparkles are not better than Weeds. Everything works in balance with everything else. A mosquito sting is bothersome to us, but it nourishes her children."

"Couldn't agree more, my dear Mother Nature," Bluster said with a respectful nod. "But a bit of competition never hurt any friendship. Why, look at us, darling. We're always playing some game or another."

Mother Nature pressed her lips together. "I suppose that's true," she said slowly.

"Oh, please let us compete," Winter begged. "We're only having fun. Besides, we might need you to judge!"

Summer gazed down at her feet. Usually, she'd be right there with Winter, begging Mother Nature to judge. But all this rivalry stuff had gone too far already.

"Yes," Autumn said quickly. "Otherwise, Bluster Tempest will be the only judge and it won't be fair!"

"I assure you I would be most fair and judicious," Bluster said, "but the young ladies do have a point, my dear."

Mother Nature hesitated. "All right," she said. "Under two conditions. One: No magic. Only your wits and skills may be used." Summer looked at Thunderbolt, who was nodding solemnly. For some reason, this made her feel a lot better about the competition.

"Two," Mother Nature continued. "You all must remember that a game is played not to prove how much better you are than someone else, but to prove how much better you are than you thought you could be." Summer felt as if Mother was looking sidelong at her, as if she could read Summer's thoughts.

"Now that the formalities are done," Bluster cried, once everyone had shaken hands and agreed upon the rules, "let's also remember that a game is good fun. Why don't we set a wager on the competition outcome, hmm? If my boys win, Mother Nature must agree to play a round of Turmoil Trivia with me."

"That's where all the questions are about earthquakes and tsunamis and such," Thunderbolt whispered to Summer. "And if you answer a question wrong, the cards go flying across the room and you have to pick them up!" Summer made a face. She could see why Mother Nature wouldn't like that.

"But if *your* girls win," Bluster continued, "you can name the game."

Mother Nature tilted her head, a slight smile on her lips that Summer had never seen before. It reminded her of how she felt when she was about to beat Winter in a kayak race to Pineapple Island.

"Deal," Mother Nature said. Bluster Tempest beamed. "Except," she added, "if *I* win, then *you* must serve us all a proper high tea. Teeny sandwiches and all!"

"Done," Bluster said.

"And . . . ," Mother Nature added, "you must wear the pink frilly dress that Serenity gave me for my birthday."

Autumn stifled a giggle. The Weeds openly cackled and Summer couldn't help but laugh. The thought of Bluster in that dress was hilarious.

"Wager accepted," Bluster cried. "Let the games begin!"

Summer studied the racecourse carefully. The glistening snow sloped lazily at first, looped around a thicket of trees, and cascaded down toward a jump before evening out in flat terrain. It then curved down a slope pocked with trees they'd have to dodge before ending at the finish line. They needed to get plenty of speed going from the jump or they'd get stuck in the flat part. She felt a hand on her shoulder and looked up. It was Thunderbolt.

"Get lots of speed from the jump," he said quietly, and walked away. Summer stared at him, puzzled. Why did he want to help her?

"Come on, Summer!" Winter was arranging Spring and Autumn in the middle of the toboggan. "Since I know the terrain the best, I'll shout orders from the back. Summer, you steer in the front. When I say, 'Left!' lean left. When I say, 'Right!' lean right. Got it?"

They nodded. The Weeds were already in their dark toboggan, Sleet in the back and Thunderbolt in the front. Summer's stomach filled with butterflies. The "Sparkles versus Weeds" aspect was making her uncomfortable. She decided she would just focus on having fun. She loved to race when she was on her own. Why should a race with her sisters and the Weeds be any different?

Bluster Tempest ambled to the side of the two competing toboggans. "Mother Nature and I really must leave for a prior engagement," he said. "I'm afraid we cannot stay to watch today's festivities. But I trust you'll all follow our little rules, hmm?"

The Sparkles and Weeds nodded. Winter and Sleet glanced at each other suspiciously.

"All right, then!" Bluster cried, and he held up a black-and-white checkered flag. "On your marks." The girls dug their hands into the snow. "Get set." Summer took a deep breath in. "Go!" He lowered the flag brusquely and the Sparkles pushed off ahead of the Weeds, the chilly wind blowing sharply in their faces.

"Left!" called Winter.

Summer leaned left. They swerved around a thicket of trees.

"Right!"

Summer leaned right. They were nearing the jump. She leaned forward to gain speed.

"Left!" Winter called. Summer hesitated. Did they need to turn left? They were going quite fast, but if

they slowed down to turn, they'd never have enough speed after the jump to make it past the flat terrain.

"Left, Summer!" Winter called again. Summer turned her head around to explain what she was thinking, but just then Autumn and Spring leaned left, jostling Summer. She wobbled and the toboggan wobbled with her.

"Ah!" she cried. She had made it worse, slowing them down so that now the Weeds were catching up. Summer caught Thunderbolt's gaze and saw that he was staring at their toboggan with a determined glint in his eyes. Was he planning to knock them over? Just then, he reached out and gave Winter a hearty push.

"Foul!" Winter called. "No shoving!" But the push had given them enough speed to soar safely over the jump and land with the acceleration they'd need to get through the flat land. Had Thunderbolt done that on purpose?

"Lousy Weed," muttered Winter. But Summer wondered if they would have made it without Thunderbolt's extra push.

"Left!" Summer leaned left and focused on her surroundings. They were navigating through a sparse forest now and would have to turn carefully. The Weeds were ahead, but there was no way to pass them directly without crashing into a tree. Sleet turned around to see how far ahead of the Sparkles they were. He grinned. Just then, Summer noticed an ice-coated rock in the Weeds' path.

"Thunderbolt, watch out!" she shouted instinctively. Sleet turned around and the Weeds swerved right, avoiding the rock by a hair's breadth. The swerve slowed them down a little bit and the

Sparkles caught up. The two toboggans left the forest at the same time and crossed the finish line in tandem.

The Weeds jumped up and cheered, mussing one another's hair. Summer bit her lip. By not following Winter's direction, had she allowed the Weeds to tie them?

Winter jumped out and marched to Summer. "What was that?"

"What?"

"Why did you help the Weeds out?"

Summer blushed. She didn't want to tell her sisters that she'd been worried that Thunderbolt might get hurt. What if they made fun of her?

"I wanted it to be a fair game," she answered.

"Thanks a lot, Sparkle! Couldn't have done it without you," Sleet shouted. He and Quake gave each other a high five.

"You didn't win," Winter shot back. "It was a tie."

"Winter, remember we have plenty of other challenges," Summer said, taking her sister's hand. She hoped a little hand squeeze could warm up her sister's attitude. "In fact, is the obstacle course ready, Autumn?"

Autumn nodded. "Whisper prepared it last night."

"Great," said Winter. "Let's go, Sparkles. The sooner we win these contests, the sooner we don't have to talk to any more Weeds."

Summer followed her sisters away from the toboggans. She wished she hadn't made Winter so mad. She felt like it was all her fault that her sisters were angry at the Weeds, when all Summer wanted was for her sisters to get along with them. Why couldn't they be friends with the Weeds, just like they were with each other? She had to help her sisters win the competition—afterward, she could prove to them that the Weeds weren't all bad.

Summer smiled resolutely as she followed her sisters on the rainbow to Autumn's realm.

CHAPTER
6

Outside Autumn's Caramel Apple Orchard, the Sparkles gathered to talk strategy. Whisper, Autumn's elephant, shyly nuzzled his giant trunk against Autumn. He had big violet eyes that glittered like amethyst gemstones beneath his dark lashes. His tough, leaf-patterned hide was pure orange, like a giant pumpkin.

"I don't see why you didn't just set up the obstacle course yourself," Winter grumbled. "It must have taken Whisper ages, what with using just his trunk and all."

Spring looked at Whisper and made a sound like a trumpet, throwing her head back. Whisper trumpeted right back. Spring's ability to talk to animals always amused Summer, especially right now, when absurd noises came out of her cute-as-a-button, ringlet-framed face.

"Whisper says it only took him a few hours. He got the squirrels to help out." A few red-furred squirrels poked their heads out between the branches of an apple tree above them. They waved at Spring, who cheerfully clucked up at them in what must have been some kind of greeting.

"So it's through this gate?" asked Winter. Whisper nodded. A tall wooden gate opened up to the Caramel Apple Orchard, where Autumn's apples grew in rows, crisp and pink, each fruit dripping with a sweet, salty caramel-like sap from the trees.

"Ew, apples," Thunderbolt shouted. "Those look *healthy.*" The Weeds sauntered toward them, kicking up dust along the trail outside the Orchard.

"I say we skip the apples and go straight for the caramel," Twister said, indicating the caramel sap dripping down the bark of the apple trees.

Whisper blew his trunk nervously and hid behind Autumn.

"Shhh," Autumn cooed, rubbing his trunk soothingly. "It's okay, Whisper. They're just boys." Whisper slowly opened his big violet eyes and peeked out from behind Autumn's shoulder, gingerly helping her onto a tree stump.

Autumn cleared her voice, her hand shaking a little. She hated public speaking, even though half the people there were her sisters and the other half were just the silly Weeds.

"Whisper and I decided," she started quietly.

"Speak up!" Quake shouted. Summer and Winter shot him a look.

Autumn cleared her voice and spoke a smidgen louder. "Whisper and I decided to make an obstacle course based not on strength or speed, but on intelligence." She paused and Whisper nudged her in support. "At the start of the course, Whisper will give you a clue that will lead you to the first obstacle. From there you follow the course, clue to clue, obstacle to obstacle. Though Spring helped him write the clues out, Whisper has designed the course and the clues so none of us has an advantage over anyone else."

Sleet and Quake snickered at that. "An *elephant* designed this contest?"

"At the end of the course," Autumn continued, "Whisper has hidden a blue ribbon. The team that grabs it first wins." Autumn stepped down quickly from the trunk and walked over to the Sparkles.

Summer's heart beat excitedly. After letting her sisters down in the toboggan race, she felt she needed to prove to them that she was taking this competition seriously. That she was on their team.

Whisper plodded over to the gate, reached with his trunk behind the big wooden sign that read "Caramel Apple Orchard," and sucked up two little slips of paper. One he carefully gave to Autumn, the other he blew toward Thunderbolt. The Sparkles crowded around Autumn. In Spring's sprawling script were written the words "Orchard Obstacle Course." Below that were instructions:

Once through the gates, wooden and brown,
only one pair of feet
may touch the ground.
Use what you find (whether hay or horse)
to win the blue ribbon
at the end of the course.

Summer looked at Autumn quizzically, who shrugged her shoulders. Whisper grabbed a checkered flag from the gates and stood between the Sparkles and Weeds, bringing it down to the ground with a flourish. They rushed to the gates.

"Remember—only one person's feet can touch the ground per team!" Winter cried.

They all stopped short at that. In front of them stood two huge bales of hay, each taller than Bluster. Each bale was hollowed out in the center so that it looked like a giant straw wheel. Farther down the lane, a broad plank hung from an oak tree—as far off the ground as the hay bales were high. On top of the plank were two red wagons, one labeled "Sparkles," the other labeled "Weeds."

"We need to roll the hay bale over to the plank," Summer realized. "Then we can climb up and reach our wagon!" But how to roll the hay without all four of them touching the ground?

"Whirligigs and wheelbarrows." Spring sighed.

"That's a great idea, Spring!" Winter said, a gleam in her eye. "We can use a wheelbarrow!"

"A wheelbarrow?" Autumn asked, confused. "All I see is a wagon."

"No!" said Winter, hopping with excitement. "I'm talking about a Sparkle wheelbarrow!"

Without a second thought, Autumn lowered herself so Spring could stand on her shoulders. Next, Winter did a handstand and Autumn grabbed hold of her. Quickly, Summer burrowed inside the hollow of the sphere of hay, squirming through the scratchy straw. A clue stuck out inside the hay, grazing her cheek. She grabbed it and poked her head and arms out the other side.

"Another clue!" she said. Autumn peered over her shoulder, and Spring leaned down like a giant vine to get a better look.

You figured out how to move
without using eight feet.
Now unhinge your minds
or you'll get beat!

Summer frowned. *Unhinge your minds.* What could that possibly mean?

From behind, Winter gave the wheel of hay a giant shove forward, then scrambled on her hands to push again. Summer went around and around inside the hay bale. It was actually pretty fun, like rolling down a hill. As the world spun around her, she saw a dark blur of figures at the starting line—the Weeds still hadn't mobilized! A big thump told Summer they had hit the plank.

"Sparkles, let's climb this hay!" Winter ordered. Summer squirmed out and pulled herself onto the top of the hay bale, jumping onto the plank where the wagons sat. Her sisters followed suit as first Winter, then Spring and Autumn shimmied up the hay. The four of them stood in a row, staring at the red wagon labeled "Sparkles." But what next? Across a pumpkin patch were two big barrels. They had the wagon right before them, but no way to get down off the plank.

"Look," Autumn said softly. "A hinge." They looked where Autumn was squatting. A thin metal hinge ran across the length of the plank. Could that be what the clue meant? Summer carefully lowered her head to look under the plank. Pinned to a black strap was a note. The next clue! She held it up and Spring whisked it from her excitedly to read aloud.

> Pull on the strap to create a ramp,
> then wheel to the barrel
> and get your head damp.
> From there you must bob
> for an apple red.
> But only one
> may dunk her head.

"Hey, Summer . . . ," Winter said.

"One step ahead of you," said Summer, pulling on the black strap dangling beneath the plank.

Immediately, another plank swung out with a click and connected with the ground, forming a wooden incline.

"Hurry up!" Winter said. Summer followed her gaze. The Weeds had copied their wheelbarrow technique and were starting to pull themselves onto the plank. All four Sparkles jumped into the wagon, Spring and Autumn on Winter's and Summer's laps.

"Wheeee!" Spring called out as Summer pushed off and the wagon flew down the ramp. Once it slowed, Summer jumped out and pulled her sisters through the pumpkin patch, weaving between the golden gourds. Ahead of them were the two barrels, one that read "Sparkles," the other labeled "Weeds." Summer hustled to their barrel. It was full of water, a few apples floating near the bottom. Autumn picked off a white note from the lip of the barrel and read it aloud.

Once the treat is in your mouth,
give a whistle to summon your mount.

What could that possibly mean? There was no time to think hard about it, as the Weeds had figured out the hinge clue and were hurtling toward their barrel. "I'll be the one who bobs for apples," Summer said.

"Maybe Autumn should," Spring said cautiously. "She's bobbed a lot before." But Summer wanted to show her sisters how committed she was to their team.

"I can do it," she said, dunking her head into the barrel of icy water. But as soon as Summer's lips touched an apple, it slipped away. She came up for air and saw that Twister had an apple in his mouth. Summer took a deep breath and dunked her head back in. This time, instead of trying to feel the apple with her lips, she bore her teeth. She felt the stem of an apple on her front tooth and opened her mouth wide, biting down hard. Quickly, before it could escape her, she brought her head up.

"Whistle, whistle!" Spring demanded, bouncing from foot to foot.

Summer waved the apple above her head and put her lips between her fingers to whistle loudly. A beautiful bay horse emerged from the cornfield and trotted toward Summer—the next step in the obstacle course! The name "Nadine" was written on her saddle.

"Hurry up!" Winter shouted. "The Weeds are already on their horse!" The horse nuzzled for the apple in Summer's hand, and as Summer petted her, her hand brushed against something smooth— the next clue! She took it off of Nadine's mane and turned to her sisters.

Only two may ride the horse from here.
The other two must stay and cheer.
Once through the maze you can have your reunion—
and win the course, by finding the ribbon.
But first make your way through the corn links
and don't forget about animal instincts.

"I'm going," Winter said. "I'm used to riding Flurry."

"I can go," Spring said. "I'm used to riding Dewdrop. And he is a horsey!" Summer's heart sank. Suddenly, Nadine neighed loudly. Spring cocked her head and furrowed her brow.

"Nadine wants Summer to go," Spring said. Summer stared at the horse. How could she know how guilty Summer felt about letting her sisters down? Nadine calmly pawed at the earth, waiting. Time was running out. The Weeds could be almost at the end of the cornfield by now.

"Let's go then, Summer!" Winter shouted. They mounted quickly and Summer gave Nadine a quick thank-you squeeze on the shoulder. The horse blew out her lips and nuzzled Summer's hand, trotting to an opening in the cornfield below a wooden board that read "Corn Maze." This was an actual maze made of cornstalks!

"A maze of maize," Summer thought aloud.

Winter looked at her sister quizzically.

"'Maize' is another word for corn," Summer said.

"Well, should we go left or right?" Winter asked.

"Let's try left." Summer pulled at the reins, but Nadine shook her head and resisted.

"Looks like Nadine doesn't want to go left," Winter said thoughtfully.

"That's it!" said Summer excitedly. "*'Animal instincts.'* This is part of the challenge! We have to trust Nadine's instincts."

The line dawned on Winter. "Of course!" she said. "From the clue!"

"Okay, girl," Summer whispered to Nadine. "You tell us which way to go."

Nadine whinnied, then took a right. All around them rose tall, green cornstalks. Summer and Winter exchanged looks. Should they really trust a horse? But neither protested.

At last, they came to an opening in the maze and out of the towering cornfield. Ahead of them was a single oak tree, thick and tall, with a slide sloping down from a high branch. Nadine stopped.

"Can you take us to the oak tree, girl?" Winter asked.

Nadine shook her head, and reached back toward the saddle horn beneath Summer's hand.

"This?" Summer asked, wiggling the horn. Nadine neighed encouragingly. Summer lifted up the saddle beneath the horn and, sure enough, found their final clue.

You have reached the end of the course.
What a lovely surprise!
The next obstacle holds the blue ribbon prize.
All you must do is slide down from the tree
And scavenge amongst a leafy sea!

Summer and Winter exchanged glances, thinking the same thing. "Only one of us can touch the ground," Summer said. She looked ahead, distracted, searching for the Weeds. They were nowhere to be found. Had they already won?

"Finally," said a nasal voice behind her. They turned. It was Sleet, riding the horse with Thunderbolt behind him.

"See," said Thunderbolt. "I told you all we needed to do was trust the horse." He and Summer met each other's eyes. For a second, Summer froze. It was a second too long.

"I'll do it," Winter shouted, and started running.

"Wait," Summer called. "Use your scepter as a pole!" But Winter couldn't hear. Summer saw a look of recognition cross Thunderbolt's eyes, and he grabbed a thick branch that had fallen on the ground. Though he couldn't pole-vault yet, he was able to use it for leverage. He slid off of the horse, sticking the branch into the ground and leaping, pushing up from the branch to gain height. He landed ahead of Winter and scrambled up the oak tree. Winter climbed up below his heels. Thunderbolt reached the slide and slid down headfirst, diving into a huge pile of crisp leaves. Winter followed. If only Summer hadn't said the pole-vaulting hint out loud! Now the Weeds had a chance to win, and it was all Summer's fault. She concentrated on the pile, trying to find the blue ribbon so she could warn her sister, but it was too late. As soon as she saw it, floating upward with the leaves after Winter's dive, Thunderbolt saw it too. He reached up and caught it with one hand. Summer gasped.

Spring, Autumn, Twister, and Quake jogged out of the maze just in time to see Thunderbolt's victory.

"Take that," Sleet whooped. "Weeds *are* better."

"Not so fast," said Spring. "We still have three more contests, and the next one is in *my* realm."

Twister rolled his eyes. "What is it, an egg-dyeing contest?"

"No," Spring said defensively. "It's a ballet race." This only made the Weeds laugh harder.

"Don't worry, Sparkles," Summer said. "We'll win this next one." But even as she said it, she doubted it was true.

Spring stood on a stool in her pink ballet slippers in front of the outdoor Daffodil Dance Studio as Dewdrop the unicorn chomped on a nearby patch of pink milk thistles.

"The rules of Ballet Relay Racing are simple," she said. "As in any relay race, each runner must sprint to the next person on the team and hand off the baton before the next runner can go. The team whose final runner crosses the finish line first wins."

"So what makes this special?" Sleet asked, gazing at the daffodils uneasily. His nose quivered, as if he were allergic to the beauty of the flowers.

"You can only do ballet moves, silly," Spring said.

"Ballet moves?" Quake snorted, his nose curling up as well. "Like—tra-la-la?" He spun around, skipping, his arms over his head.

"Sort of," Spring said. "You can only move forward through *pas de chat*, *chassé*, *assemblé en tournant*, *glissade*, *jeté*, and *pirouette*." As she spoke, she jumped off the stool, displaying the movements.

"You mean *jumping*?" Twister said with a guffaw. "Yeah, we know how to jump."

"Good," Spring said. "Then you shouldn't have any trouble doing *jetés* in these." She handed out seven pairs of pink ballet slippers. "And remember," she added, "ballet is often done on your toes. If you run using any other part of your feet, you will be disqualified."

"So basically," Sleet said, "all we have to do is run in these pink shoes while turning and jumping?"

Spring nodded. Basically, that was it.

"Awesome!" Twister said. "This is the easiest contest ever!" Winter and Summer looked at each other. Why couldn't Spring have thought of something a bit more challenging? But Spring didn't seem bothered.

Once everyone was in their slippers, they spread out through the two gravelly race lanes cleared of daffodils: Winter first, then Autumn, then Summer, then Spring. The Weeds goofily followed, Quake starting out with the baton next to Winter.

After everyone was settled in place, Dewdrop cantered in between Quake and Winter, a checkered flag in his teeth. With dignity, he brought it down. Winter and Quake were off, both going for speed. But while Quake stuck to running on his toes, Winter took long, graceful jumps and turns that brought her quickly to Autumn. Autumn was not as fast as Winter, but looked so elegant turning that Summer almost started clapping when Autumn got to her. But there was no time. Summer leaped and lunged from one toe to the other, using her arms to propel herself forward like she would if she were swimming in the sea.

Out of the corner of her eye, she saw Thunderbolt next to her gaining speed. She almost laughed. He looked so silly, spinning and turning in his pink slippers. They handed off their batons at the same time—Summer to Spring, Thunderbolt to Sleet. Sleet grinned wildly, then started running. It was clear right away that he had underestimated the difficulty of running in ballet slippers. He faltered, his stride shortening as his face reddened and his breath quickened. Spring, meanwhile, easily glided across the gravel path. When she jumped, it looked like the wind itself was catching her up and carrying her forward. She crossed the finish line before Sleet could even hand off the baton to Twister. She threw the baton up in an ornamental twirl and the girls broke out in applause.

"You guys didn't even give me a chance!" called Twister. He jumped, spinning in the air and landing right into a backward handspring. The Sparkles' jaws dropped. Of all the adjectives to describe Twister, "graceful" was not the first to come to mind.

Thunderbolt jogged up to Summer, still wearing his slippers. He nodded toward Twister and cupped his hands to his mouth.

"Show-off!" he called. Then he leaned into Summer. "Think Spring will let me keep these?" he asked. "I lost my basketball sneakers." Summer laughed at the thought of Thunderbolt playing basketball in delicate ballet slippers.

"Only if you pirouette before you dunk," said Summer. She mimicked the move and Thunderbolt burst into guffaws.

"Nice steering with the toboggan race," he said to her. "I would have eaten ice if you hadn't helped us out."

"Thanks," she said. "Nice vaulting with the branch."

He grinned at her and winked. "It was no pole-vault," he said.

"Hey," Winter said, staring at the two of them. "No talking to the competition! Come on, Summer. We've got a big day tomorrow. We need to rest up if we're going to win both afternoon contests, and we need to. We're tied with the Weeds right now. One to one."

Summer blushed and looked at the ground. She hadn't meant to make Winter angry. Wasn't there a way she could prove to her sisters that she loved them without totally ignoring Thunderbolt? It had been a long, exhausting day. With a sharp jolt, she realized that the two contests that they'd have tomorrow would be in the Weeds' realm—the Barrens—and her own. Yikes. She had a lot to do to prepare. Now if only she could skip tomorrow altogether.

CHAPTER
7

Summer woke up the next morning to a cloudless sky. It was a perfect summer day for sailing. And if there was one thing that could lift Summer's spirits from yesterday's races, it was sailing. She hopped into her green tankini and white shorts and slid down the banister of her spiral staircase that wrapped around the outside of the ceiba trees all the way down to the roots. The ever-blossoming pink blooms on the trees swirled as she spiraled down, becoming a pink blur to her green eyes. Summer landed on Shade's waiting back, hugging the jaguar's neck.

"To the boat dock!" she cried, and Shade raced down the pebbled path that wove down to the beach, where a stony dock stretched over the clear blue water. She loped past the boats until they were nose-to-bow with a bright green sailboat named

Birdy. Its beak-like bow perched sprightly on the water like a chipper little sparrow. With any luck, it would be fierce and bold like a sparrow too.

Summer squealed with delight. "It looks small but fast," she said. "Like me!" She clambered in and Shade followed. She had designed the boat for her sisters. She wanted it to be fast, easy to sail, but also fun and entertaining, in case Spring or Autumn got bored in the middle of the Sparkle Sea. She was dying to test it out before their race that afternoon.

"Hey," a voice said behind her. "I'm here for my pole-vaulting lesson."

Summer looked up. Thunderbolt was standing on the dock, wearing flip-flops and long black swimming trunks with purple lightning bolts up the sides. She hesitated. Would she be betraying her sisters by letting Thunderbolt sail with her? Then again, it was better to sail with two people—one steering with the tiller, the other manning the sails.

"Hop in," she said. "Come try out this new boat with me first." Thunderbolt leaped off the dock into the boat with a thud that set them rocking. "Be careful!" she said, but Thunderbolt laughed with such a huge grin on his face that Summer couldn't help but smile too.

"As long as we get around to pole-vaulting at some point."

"We'll get to it," she said, still smiling. "First, untie that rope from the dock. But be careful not to—"

Thunderbolt was already standing at the edge of the bow, balancing precariously as he untied the rope and pushed off from the dock.

"Okay," Summer said. "I'm going to turn the boat into the wind, so I need you to pull in the mainsail. Make sure to duck when the boom comes around."

"What's the boom?" he said, ducking just in time as the heavy log swung around. Shade burrowed into the deepest part of the hull with a yelp and put her paws over her head.

"Aaaand that must be the boom." Thunderbolt laughed good-naturedly. Summer giggled.

"Just keeping you on your toes," she said. "Now loosen up the mainsail and we'll make this boat fly." The sail caught the wind and the boat skipped cheerfully across the water. Shade relaxed and peered over the boat, pawing at the water for fish. Thunderbolt was a quick learner, good at anticipating how much wind the boat needed, and calm—very important for a sailing partner. Summer always had to soothe Winter when she got frustrated at the boom, but Thunderbolt didn't seem nervous about anything.

"Let's stop here," he said. To their left was a mossy island with parrots and howling monkeys that Shade liked to chase up trees.

"At the island?" she asked.

"No," he said. "Right here." And he began to jump from one foot to the other, rocking the boat.

"Quit it." She laughed. "You'll capsize us." He grinned at her.

"So?" he said, and jumped even harder.

"Thunderbolt! St—" The boat went under. The water was as warm as a Jacuzzi. When she surfaced, the boat had bobbed back upright. Thunderbolt pulled himself up into the boat and then lent a hand to Shade, who sulked onto the boat and shook out her dark mane of fur, gasping dramatically. Summer laughed. Thunderbolt caught her gaze. He dove back into the water and shot toward her like a shark. She dropped below him. When he surfaced, uncertain where she'd gone, she tugged his foot.

"That's what I was going to do!" he cried.

"Duh! I've been doing that to Winter since we were six!"

Just then, a rainbow whirred and warbled by Summer. Her Sparkle Sisters were calling her.

"I have to go," she said, a little sad to leave. She was having so much fun!

"Why?" asked Thunderbolt.

"Because. My sisters are calling me."

"So? You'll see them later. You owe me a pole-vaulting lesson. Remember?"

Summer hesitated. She'd never ignored a call from her sisters before. But she'd also never broken a promise. "Do your brothers know you're here?" she asked Thunderbolt. He looked away and reddened.

"Yeah," he said. "They're not too happy about it. They wanted to dig up ants to make an ant farm, but I told them I was going to go to your realm to practice pole-vaulting."

"Did they make fun of you?"

"Yeah," he said, "but I don't care." She could tell by the way he puffed out his chest that he did care, though. "It's silly how angry our siblings get," he said carefully, "just because we're friends." Summer smiled at the word. They were *friends*. That did it. She decided to ignore the rainbow. She had made a promise to her friend, and you don't break promises to friends.

"Time to pole-vault. Race you to the boat!" she cried.

"No fair!" shouted Thunderbolt, swimming behind her.

✳

"I can't do it," Thunderbolt said. He dropped his pole and slumped onto the sand. They were standing on the beach practicing pole-vaulting as Shade napped in the sun. Thunderbolt had almost landed his jump, but after an hour, he still hadn't done it successfully. Summer wasn't about to let him quit, though. Not yet.

"You're doing great," she said, deciding to try a different tactic. "Do a push-up," she said.

He groaned. "How about you give me an 'E' for effort and we call it a day?"

She smiled. "Do a push-up!"

"All right, all right." Thunderbolt grumbled, but he rolled onto his stomach and pushed up. Summer brought the pole to him.

"Now reach up with your left hand and grab the pole." He did. "Now grab with your right hand."

"But—"

"Do it!" she ordered. Quickly, he lifted his left hand, and before his body could fall, instinctively grabbed on with his right hand. He was balancing nearly his entire body weight on the pole. "This is the grip you need to maintain as you run, lift, and jump with your pole. Stand up while keeping the grip."

He did so.

"Now try to jump," she said, and folded her arms.

She thought Thunderbolt was going to argue again, but instead he frowned, a determined crease deepening between his brows. Suddenly, he sprinted to the line she'd drawn in the sand, planted his pole, and lifted off, keeping his grip tight until his feet reached directly above his head and then shot out in front of him in a perfect arc. He landed on his feet and turned to her, a triumphant grin on his face.

"You did it!" she exclaimed, and ran toward him, jumping to give him a satisfyingly loud high five.

"Only because you taught me," he said. "You're a great coach." She blushed. It sounded so grown-up—to be a good coach. Teaching Thunderbolt how to pole-vault felt even better than pole-vaulting herself.

"I just like to share what I love with friends," she said.

"Me too," he said. He was panting and sweating, but was clearly pleased with himself.

Summer smiled. She knew exactly how he felt. Suddenly, a tiny twister buzzed around Thunderbolt's head. He slapped at it as if it were an annoying fly. It buzzed against his ear.

"Ugh, quit it!" he said, but held out his hand, as if for a piece of gum. The twister hovered above his palm and deposited a note.

"Come home," he said, reading the terse message. He crumpled it up and threw it at the mini twister, which sucked it up and buzzed away. Summer looked at him curiously. "My brothers," Thunderbolt explained. "I guess they're getting impatient. They probably want to practice before the contest at the Barrens. See you soon?" he said, standing up.

"Yeah!" Summer said. "Definitely!"

Thunderbolt grinned. "Awesome! Remember—don't wear anything you care about to the Barrens."

"Yeah," said Summer. "I kind of figured."

Thunderbolt smiled and waved. "Good-bye, friend."

"Good-bye, Weed," Summer said with a smile as she watched Thunderbolt conjure a storm cloud and vanish into it.

Summer wondered what kind of contest the Weeds would host in the Barrens. Even though she wasn't allowed to do magic, she might need her scepter. She used her scepter for all kinds of things aside from magic. She reached out for her scepter on the sand where she'd left it and noticed it wasn't there. Where was it? Her mouth went dry.

She saw Thunderbolt's pole there, and the line she drew in the sand was still there, but no scepter. Her stomach sank. Did Thunderbolt steal it?

"He didn't, right, Shade?"

Shade growled uncertainly. Had Thunderbolt tricked her? Had he faked their whole friendship? Her mind raced. Summer buried her face in Shade's warm fur. She wanted her sisters. Just then, she heard chiming laughter from the dock. It was as if her sisters could read her mind. She sighed with relief and ran over to where they were sitting on the dock. They stopped laughing when they saw her face.

"Summer, what's wrong?" Autumn asked softly.

"Your face looks as red as a beet and watermelon salad!" Spring said.

"It looks blotchy," Winter said.

Summer tried to shrug it off like it was no big deal. "Thunderbolt visited me today. I thought maybe he wanted to pole-vault with me, but I guess he came to steal my scepter, because it's gone now."

"Oh, no!" Spring said, looking around at her sisters. "That sounds just like something Thunderbolt would do!"

"You poor thing," Winter said. "You just can't trust those Weeds."

At the word "trust," Summer burst into tears. She tried to hold it in, but couldn't. Shade stood protectively at her feet. "I'm sorry, Sparkles," she said. "I don't know why I'm getting so emotional."

Autumn put her arm around Summer and gave her a gold-embroidered handkerchief. "It's okay to cry," she said soothingly. "Let it out."

"It's just . . . ," Summer said, hiding her runny nose in the cloth, "I thought we were friends." She started sobbing so much she couldn't even speak.

"You'll get it back," Winter said. "We'll make sure to get it back after the contests." But Summer wasn't upset because she'd lost her scepter. She was upset because she'd lost her friend. And that hurt more than scraping her knee on birch bark, more than getting a grass burn, more than a jellyfish sting, more than any kind of hurt she'd felt before.

CHAPTER
8

Summer and her sisters walked slowly over a dark asphalt path in the Barrens. Along the path, sheets of steel rose high, ending in curls of barbed wire.

Winter scrunched up her face. "It smells like old sweaty socks here."

Autumn closed her eyes and took a deep breath. "If you breathe in deeply, you'll acclimate."

Winter coughed. "Or you'll faint," she said. "Though at least then you wouldn't smell it."

Ahead, the path ended at a swamp the size of a football field. The Weeds stood at its edge, punching one another in the arms. In the middle of their circle, a little black Tasmanian devil snapped at his own tail with his teeth. Thunderbolt had told Summer about him—his name was Bedlam and he was a fierce little guy who growled menacingly at strangers. But once you gained his trust, he was loyal to you forever. From speakers attached to telephone poles, loud heavy-metal music blared. When Thunderbolt saw Summer, he grinned and jaunted over. Autumn gently squeezed her hand in support. Summer took a deep breath and set her face into a neutral expression.

"Summer!" he shouted. "Look at this!" He pointed at the swamp. "It's a giant mud pit! This is going to be so fun. Let me show you." Before Summer could protest, he took her hand, pulling her over to a wooden deck, which they hopped up on. She glanced back to see her sisters' horrified faces.

"See the rock-climbing wall?" Thunderbolt said. "You have to be careful which rocks you touch, because the shiny black ones squirt mud at you! Then at the top we've got eight all-terrain vehicles. VROOOM! Then you have to climb up that mud slope and slide down to the tire course. If your leg touches the inside of the tire, a cardboard zombie pops out in front of you! Spoooky! Then see that trampoline at the end? Whoever jumps high enough to grab the flag wins!" He grinned and paused for breath. "What do you think?"

Summer looked away. "It's fine, Thunderbolt," she said. "Good job." She started to walk back toward her sisters.

"Geez," he said. "What's gotten into you? Why are you acting so . . . boring?" The word stung the back of her neck like a wasp. Summer whirled around, red-faced.

"First you steal my scepter, then you call me boring? At least I don't pretend to be someone's friend when I'm not!" Thunderbolt stared at her for a moment, his brow creased in what looked like confusion.

"I didn't steal your scepter," he said. "Why would I want your dumb scepter?"

"It's not dumb, and stop lying. You and your brothers always steal stuff from us, and it went missing right after you left my Sparkledom. I thought you might be different from them, but I guess I was wrong. Once a Weed, always a Weed."

Thunderbolt's face grew red with anger. "So what if I'm a Weed? I like being a Weed. We play outside and do whatever we want while you Sparkles sit in your little houses, too worried about getting your dresses dirty to have any fun."

Summer turned and stormed off to her sisters.

"I didn't steal your scepter, but now I wish I had!" he called after her.

"Don't listen to that silly Weed," Winter said. "He's just trying to make you mad before the race to psych you out."

"I'm not mad. I don't care what he says," Summer said, loud enough for Thunderbolt to hear. "When this race is over, I'll just ask Mother to make him give my scepter back." From the corner of her eye, she saw Thunderbolt's jaw tighten before he jumped from the deck and marched over to his brothers.

"Come on," he said loudly. "Let's get this over with and cream these silly Sparkles." His brothers whooped in agreement.

Bedlam snarled and pointed his rodent-like snout at the sky, baring his sharp teeth.

"Aw," Spring said. "He's so cute!" Before Summer could stop her, Spring was squatting down next to Bedlam, sniffing his dribbling snout. To their amazement, Bedlam playfully swatted at Spring with his paw, making a noise that sounded close to laughter. Spring swatted right back.

"He says it's time to start the obstacle course!" Spring yelped, and jumped to her feet, Bedlam now rubbing his head against her shin in adoration.

"I'll never get used to Spring's comfort with scary animals," Autumn murmured. Winter and Summer nodded.

The two groups gathered in front of the swamp and Thunderbolt repeated the instructions.

Summer tried to pay attention, but she couldn't stop seething. She looked at her sisters and saw they were relaxed, even excited. *Maybe it's a good thing I feel so mad*, she thought. Maybe she could turn her anger into energy for the race.

She followed her sisters as they gathered to the right of Bedlam. At least they'd been listening. She'd just have to follow their lead until she got the hang of things.

With the checkered flag clenched in his jaw, Bedlam stood on his hind legs between the two groups—Weeds to the left, Sparkles to the right. With a squirming jump, he brought the flag up and then down to the ground. The game had begun.

Summer and her sisters jumped into the swamp and started slogging through the waist-high muck to the rock-climbing wall up ahead. The Weeds were laughingly throwing mud at one another and diving through the murk. Summer narrowed her brows and tried to run, but it was difficult to move. Suddenly, Spring dove into the mud. She came out ten feet ahead, looking like a melting Fudgsicle.

"Swim through it!" she shouted. "It's easier!" Autumn and Winter quickly joined, rising near Spring like swamp monsters, their hair dripping goopily. Summer glared at Thunderbolt before diving in as well. She bet he designed this course purposely to humiliate her and her sisters.

Spring hit the rock-climbing wall first, followed by Twister, Thunderbolt, and Winter. Summer propelled herself forward up the wall. *SPLAT.* Mud ejected from the wall onto her face.

"Don't touch the shiny black rocks," Winter called down from on top of the wall. Too late.

At the top of the wall, Spring, Twister, Winter, and Thunderbolt were already strapping themselves into their vehicles. Twister shot off first, zooming straight down the first hill, leaving a trail of smoky dust. Summer jumped into a vehicle shortly after Autumn, putting the key in the ignition and pressing hard on the gas. *VROOOM*. Her vehicle shot off . . . in reverse! Autumn turned to see what had happened and swiftly stopped her car. Quake zoomed off ahead of them.

"Are you okay, Summer?" Autumn called. "Didn't you hear what Thunderbolt said about turning the key to the left first . . ."

"Go! I'm fine!" she shouted to Autumn, not wanting her to fall behind. They both raced over the hills, and Summer was determined not to make any more silly mistakes. She watched Spring and Winter jump from their cars and scramble up a giant sloping bouncy mountain, mud gushing down at them.

Autumn smiled at Summer broadly. "More mud!" she said.

Summer realized that Autumn was actually enjoying this! The idea that she was the only one not having fun put Summer in an even worse temper. She clawed bitterly at the bouncy mountain, each muddy grasp slipping out of her hands, sending her into a deeper funk.

"Come on," Autumn said, holding out her hand from above. "Grab on!" Summer grabbed hold and Autumn pulled her up. It was time for her to put her frustration at Thunderbolt aside and focus—if not for herself, then for her sisters' sake. "Okay," Summer said, forcing a smile. "Let's slide!"

"That's the Summer I know!" Autumn shouted. Together, they held hands and slid down the muddy slide. At the bottom was the tire course Thunderbolt had mentioned. They had to jump from tire to tire without touching the inner rubber—if they did, a cardboard zombie would pop up in front of them, slowing them down. Summer hopped from one tire to the other, Autumn following a little more cautiously. They picked up speed and passed Quake and Twister. Finally, they caught up to Spring, Winter, Sleet, and Thunderbolt jumping on two separate trampolines, a red flag dangling high above each. It was the final obstacle. Whoever jumped high enough to grab the flag would win the course for their team. Thunderbolt and Sleet were roughhousing on the trampoline, each trying to outdo the other. It looked like they weren't even trying to get the flag. Spring jumped gracefully, Winter forcefully, her eyes glued on the flag. Summer relaxed. Winter would surely get it.

Suddenly, Sleet landed hard on the Weeds' trampoline, right as Thunderbolt started to jump. Thunderbolt went catapulting high into the trees. He reached out easily and grabbed the flag, hurtling back down onto the trampoline in a curled-up ball. It was over. The Weeds had won the course. If Summer hadn't been so angry and fallen behind, maybe she could have been the one to catapult Spring.

"We won!" Sleet shouted. He chest-bumped Twister while Quake jumped and hooted.

"Weeds are better than Sparkles!" Quake hollered.

"You only won by accident—you weren't even trying!" Winter retorted.

"Still means we won," Sleet taunted. "Right, Thunderbolt?" But Thunderbolt wasn't listening. He had stormed off to the Barrens Castle with his hands in his pockets and a moody, glowering expression.

"What's the matter with him?" Twister asked.

Sleet shrugged. "Probably needs to blow chunks after all that jumping," he said. "We did eat a lot of chocolate worms for breakfast."

"Gross," said Winter with a glare, but that only made them tease the Sparkles *more*.

Summer felt her face getting hot and her throat starting to tighten. She didn't want the Weeds to know how upset she was over a silly game. Autumn, Spring, and Winter huddled around her protectively, twining their arms so that Summer felt like she was in a safe little cove made of her Sparkle Sisters.

"It's okay, Summer," Winter said soothingly. "It's two to one. There's still a chance we'll tie and then do a tiebreaker. A big chance, actually, since the race is in *your* kingdom. We're *bound* to win that one!"

Summer tried to smile. Normally, she'd be so excited to sail in her kingdom on a sunny, calm day. She wished she could go back to this morning, when it was just her and Thunderbolt, sailing together and goofing off. But how could she wish to go back to this morning if her friendship with Thunderbolt had been nothing more than a lie? Summer bit her lip and bent her head into the crook of her arms. From a tight place in her chest, she felt the hot tears rising.

CHAPTER
9

After everyone had cleaned off the muck from the Barrens in the bubbly hot springs in Summer's Sparkledom, they headed over to the dock. The beautiful sunny day did not reflect the Sparkles' inner turmoil.

"Sure you're okay to steer?" Winter asked, sitting down next to Summer in their new boat, *Birdy*. Autumn and Spring gazed at her from their side seats. Summer nodded and forced a smile. If she couldn't make her Sparkledom reflect her mood, maybe she could make her mood reflect her Sparkledom.

"I won't let my frustration with Thunderbolt get to me this time," Summer assured her sisters. She looked over at the Weeds' sailboat, which looked more like a Viking ship than anything else. The sails were striped and torn at the edges. The bow was shaped like the head of a sea dragon, and the stern was its whiplike tail. Thunderbolt hung from the top of the mast with one hand while his brothers climbed up from the bottom like squirrels.

"You bozos ready?" Winter called to the Weeds.

In response, the Weeds hoisted a flag. It was dark and mottled, featuring the slogan "Sparkles Stink!"

"I wish we'd thought of making a flag," Summer said wistfully. Maybe if she hadn't wasted her time with Thunderbolt that morning, she would have had time to make one.

"I brought something that might work," Autumn said modestly. She held up a giant crocheted scarf. Little silver stars twinkled in the background behind the simple phrase "Sparkles Shine." The girls cheered and squeezed Autumn into a Sparkle sandwich.

"It's perfect." Summer beamed. They raised it up to the masthead. It undulated elegantly in the breeze. Shade bounded up the dock from the beach. It was time for the final game to begin. Summer stood up and gave the instructions. It was quite simple—they were to race across the Sparkle Sea to Sea Glass Island. Whichever team reached the island first won. Summer handed the checkered flag to Shade, who took it deftly in her feline teeth. With a regal nod of her head, the boats were off.

Summer called out directions to Spring and Autumn, who were manning the sails, while Winter scanned the area for rocks, sandbars, and other obstructions they had to avoid. Summer noted with satisfaction that they communicated well, listening to one another and calling out as they completed a task. Ninety percent of smooth sailing was simply good teamwork. The Weeds, on the other hand, yelled at one another snippily, each focused on his own idea of what the boat should do. The Sparkles easily sailed past them.

"Sandbar to the right!" Winter called. Summer followed Winter's gaze. A murky strip of water signaled that shallow sand lay beneath.

"Tighten the sails, I'm steering to the left," Summer called. Autumn and Spring dutifully brought in the sails. The boat skipped cheerfully away from the sandbar. Right as they were straightening out, Summer heard a yelp from the Weed boat.

"Argh!" Sleet shouted. Thunderbolt pushed the till quickly to avoid the sandbar. Their boat jolted away from the sand—and straight toward the Sparkles! Spring and Autumn cried out fearfully.

"Give up some slack," Summer called, and dexterously maneuvered the boat around the Weeds, avoiding a crash. Quake and Twister laughed gleefully. Apparently, they found the near-collision hilarious.

"Again!" Quake called. "Let's get 'em!" Thunderbolt's eyes locked on Summer's grimly. A sly smile crossed his face.

"Tighten up!" he called. His brothers hooted. Again, their boat aimed straight at the Sparkles.

"Quit it!" Winter called to them. Sleet laughed.

Sea Glass Island was in sight now. Its pale pastel shards glimmered in the sunlight, hardly different from the water that lapped against it. Summer saw Autumn clutch her stomach. Poor Autumn. All this turning must have made her seasick. They were only a minute away now, but she would need her sister's full attention to beat the Weeds.

"Crackers and ginger ale are beneath your seat," Summer called to Autumn. "It'll help. I promise."

Autumn nodded and stood up. Right as she did, Summer noticed something rising from the sea behind her. A rock! With the boys distracting them, none of them had seen that they were heading straight toward a huge jagged boulder. Instinctively, Summer pushed the till the other way. She saw everything in quick succession: Autumn, still standing, struggling to gain footing as the boom swung straight toward her stomach. It was useless to call out—Autumn was still too off balance to duck. Instinctively, Summer chanted:

"Gush of water, forceful geyser,
Spout straight at that beam of wood.
Strike it from my seasick sister
Before it hurts her for good!"

Summer held out her hands before she remembered—her scepter was gone! Her spell couldn't work without her scepter! Suddenly, from the back of Winter's coat, a powerful column of water shot straight out between Autumn and the boom. It hit the boom straight on, swinging it back around, away from Autumn. Summer ducked to avoid the blast, which propelled the boat forward, accelerating them toward Sea Glass Island. Winter turned around in shock. How had that happened?

"Look!" Sleet cried. "The Sparkles are cheating! They're using magic to create a motor!"

Before Summer could explain the strange circumstances, and how she had only meant to save Autumn, the Weeds had taken out their gnarled wands and were shouting.

"*Zhoooshlitzphat . . . Optilongvaaahn . . . xilerachijacklephap . . . shweeedlelictshundylil . . .*"

Four lines of black fog shot from the wands of Quake, Twister, Sleet, and Thunderbolt. They collided over the Sparkles' heads, tangling and dropping like stones into the sea. The Weeds exchanged glances. Clearly, this had never happened before. Summer looked over the side of the boat to see if she could watch the nasty fog sinking. The four currents of fog seemed to be chasing one another in the water, forming a spiral. She gasped.

"That's funny," Spring said softly, inspecting the water. "It looks like a—"

"WHIRLPOOL!" Winter shouted. Summer pushed the till to get away from it, but it was too late. Their boat was being sucked in.

Ahead, the Weeds were gaining on Sea Glass Island. *In thirty seconds, they'll be at the shore, and we'll be churning at the bottom of the sea*, Summer thought.

She looked helplessly over at the Weeds' boat. How to get there? Suddenly, one of the Weeds pulled their boat's tall mast from its fixture, hopped to the stern, and started running back the length of the boat. Summer tried to see who it was, but the whirlpool was spinning them faster and faster. As the figure flung himself from the back of the Weeds' boat, the mast diving straight down in the water, digging into the sand deep beneath, Summer realized who it was.

Thunderbolt's body flipped upside-down 180 degrees. He vaulted from the pole, now stuck in the water, and cleared the space between it and the Sparkles' boat. He landed in front of Summer as the boat began to twirl faster toward the doomed center.

"Hop on," he shouted, pulling out his wand. A dark fluffy cloud shot from it. The cloud hovered solidly over their heads. Summer grabbed on to the cloud, pulling herself up and calling to her sisters. Winter and Spring pushed the weakened Autumn up, then clambered onto the thundercloud with Summer's help. Just as the boat tipped down into the void, Thunderbolt hopped up with the girls. They watched the boat get sucked in and vanish before their eyes.

"Hold tight," Thunderbolt said. "I can't sustain this for long!" Summer watched anxiously as Thunderbolt focused on the Weeds' boat. She could see sweat pouring down his temples as he strained to keep all five of them afloat. Beneath her, she felt the cloud thinning and waning. They were within a few feet of the Weeds' boat when the cloud jolted.

"Ack!" Winter cried. Summer watched in terror as the part of the cloud where her sisters sat crumbled. Winter, Autumn, and Spring dropped straight into the angry, churning sea. Immediately, a blue stream burst from the Weeds' boat. Twister stood, his wand aimed at Autumn.

"*Slooooshwhiiip*," he cried. A gust of wind carried Autumn up and blew her back toward the Weeds' boat. Twister caught her safely in his arms and put her on the seat beside him.

"Help!" cried a voice from the water. Winter and Spring were bobbing up and down, taking in huge gulps of water every time a wave rolled beneath them.

"Try to duck under the waves!" Summer called. She knew from practice that it was better to dive into rather than over a large wave. Winter dove through, but Spring hesitated, fearful of going through the nasty water, and got pulled deep into the wave. Before she could even think it over,

Summer closed her eyes, put her arms up above her head, pictured the steady stream of a waterfall coursing straight down to the bottom, and jumped. The icy water enveloped and numbed her foot to head, wrapping around her like a blanket of snow. She blew bubbles from her nose to keep water from getting up and pushed her arms down to her sides, propelling her body to the surface in one swift motion. Above the water, she gasped for breath, scanning the choppy surface for her sisters. She saw Spring, her legs beating the water to keep herself buoyed. A bright red rescue tube landed in the water beside Summer. She looked back and saw Quake, his arm around another one. She made eye contact and nodded.

"Hang tight, Spring," she called, grabbing on to the tube. "I'm coming!" Summer swam as fast as she could to Spring in swift freestyle strokes. "Grab on," she said, and threw Spring the tube. Spring wrapped her arms around it tightly, breathing heavily. "Now for Winter," Summer said, determined to get her sisters to safety. "But where is she?"

"Look," Spring shouted. Summer turned just in time to see Thunderbolt high-dive into the water. He resurfaced and grabbed the rescue tube that Quake threw him, heading in the opposite direction from Summer and Spring. Summer saw Winter bobbing in the water, diving dutifully through the waves, hardly catching her breath before another one came. Thunderbolt sped toward her. Summer inhaled deeply as a wave curled and crashed over her head. When she resurfaced, Thunderbolt had one arm around Winter, fixing her into place on the tube. Summer sighed with relief. Without time to think about why Thunderbolt had helped to save her sister, she turned her attention back to her own rescue mission.

"Hold tight," Summer instructed Spring again. Spring nodded and hugged the tube tightly. Summer tied the attached rope to her waist, then swam as hard as she could, bringing her arms over her head in strong, even strokes.

When they reached the boat, Sleet pulled them up, towels at the ready. He wrapped them tight, then dashed to the back to do the same for Thunderbolt and Winter.

Summer and Autumn immediately formed their own little cocoon around Spring, squeezing her little shivering body tight.

"I'm okay. Really!" Spring managed to say through her chattering teeth.

"You were so brave, Spring," Autumn told her with another squeeze.

"So was Summer," Spring answered. "Nice high-dive, by the way."

Summer frowned quizzically at Spring. Did the seawater get to her brain? What was her little sister talking about? Then it hit her. She had high-dived off the cloud! She'd done it, without even thinking! Summer beamed and squeezed Spring's arm tenderly.

"Thanks," she said.

Thunderbolt slumped in beside Summer, shaking water from his shaggy hair.

"Yeah, nice high-dive, Summer," he said. "Though of course, you couldn't have done it without my instruction."

"And your vault wouldn't have been nearly as smooth without mine," she shot back. They smiled at each other. Thunderbolt opened his mouth to say something else, but right then, the boat hit shore.

"We're here!" Quake cried. "Finally!"

"Congratulations," Winter said, trying as hard as she could not to sound bitter.

"For what?" Sleet asked.

"For winning, duh," Winter said. "Your boat just hit Sea Glass Island."

"True," Sleet said. "But it's got both Weeds *and* Sparkles in it." Sleet gave a small smile, raised his eyebrows, and shrugged. "I guess that means it's a tie," he said.

Winter beamed. "A tie!" she shouted. "Sparkles, it's a tie!"

"Let's celebrate!" said Summer. "I'll warm us up with some magic and then we can all grab smoothies at the Sea Glass Cabana!"

"But, Summer," Autumn said, perplexed. "You don't have your scepter."

Summer shrugged. "It worked on the boat!" And before anyone else could argue, she put her hands out.

> "Heat, sizzle, bake, and fry,
> Warm us up and make us dry!"

Suddenly, something loosened and shot out from Winter's pocket, straight into Summer's hand. It was her scepter! But how had it gotten into Winter's pocket?

Winter, Autumn, and Spring all exchanged sheepish glances.

"Oh, tulips and tea trees," Spring blurted, wringing her hands. "*We're* the ones who stole your scepter, Summer. Please forgive us."

"We're sorry," Autumn whispered.

Winter stared at the ground, her face burning. "We only did it because we thought Thunderbolt was up to no good, and we didn't want him to hurt you," she said quickly.

"Yes. We're so sorry we caused you so much worry and pain."

"We know now that the Weeds are as friendly and sweet as baby porcupines," Spring chirped. "After all, they *did* save us."

Summer sighed. It felt good to hold her scepter in her hands again. She hugged it tight, and then she brought her sisters in for an even tighter hug.

"Of course I forgive you," she said, embracing them as fiercely as she would Shade. From behind their blissful cocoon, a voice coughed.

"Ahem," said Thunderbolt. The Sparkles startled apart. "I believe somebody *else* is owed an apology."

"We're sorry we blamed it on you," Winter said earnestly. "We know now that you'd never hurt our sister. You're a good guy. All of you Weeds are. As weird as that is to say."

Summer laughed. She knew what Winter meant. It was the nicest thing she'd ever heard Winter say about the Weeds.

"So we're friends?" Thunderbolt asked Summer. "Do you trust me now?" His eyes searched hers.

After a pause, she nodded. But she couldn't keep herself from adding, "Though I'd still put money on a Sparkle to beat a Weed at a sailboat race."

Thunderbolt laughed. "Come on, everybody," he shouted. "We all won, despite the craziest odds ever—including potential death by whirlpool. And I've got a great idea for how to celebrate . . ."

His eyes gleamed with mischief, and he motioned for Summer to come close so he could tell her his plan. Summer couldn't wait to hear what her friend had in mind.

The Weeds and Sparkles sat together with Mother Nature at a table adorned with flowers in her tea garden.

"Is the tea ready yet?" Mother Nature called from the table.

"Patience, love, patience," a deep voice grumbled from the kitchen.

Mother Nature winked at her Sparkles, who giggled mischievously. The kitchen door swung open.

"Tea is served," Bluster said miserably. He wore a pink petticoat that came down to his elbows and knees, and over that a lace apron with frills accessorizing the neckline and cuffs.

The Weeds laughed gleefully. Though they'd agreed the competition was a tie, they made the Sparkles promise to back them up when they told Bluster that they'd lost. They wanted to see Bluster in a frilly tea outfit. As Bluster hunched over each of them, gingerly pouring tea into their delicate cups, Mother Nature beamed at the Sparkles and Weeds. It seemed to Summer that she somehow guessed that the boys had said they'd lost for the sake of sharing some fun with the Sparkles. She got the feeling that Mother Nature approved— even though it was at her friend Bluster's expense.

"It's so lovely to have you boys over for tea," Mother Nature said warmly. "You really must come more often."

"Gee, thanks," Twister said through a mouthful of pink tea cake. "We'll definitely take you up on that."

"Absolutely," Sleet said, flicking a sugar cube into the air and angling his head just right to catch it in his mouth.

Mother Nature didn't seem put off by the Weeds' less-than-perfect manners at all. In fact, she laughed heartily. She reached out for Summer's hand to her right and Thunderbolt's hand to her left. "It truly is a victory," she said, "when you can put your losses behind you and celebrate the new things you've gained. Right, Summer?"

Summer smiled. Again, it felt like Mother Nature was reading her mind.

"As Spring will surely tell you," Mother Nature continued, "sometimes you need a few weeds to help your garden grow."

Spring nodded seriously. "Weeds hold topsoil and protect plants from getting eaten by insects. I think some are even prettier than peonies! There's ragweed, and dandelion, and cockleburs, and gold-enrod . . ."

As Spring's list went on, Summer noticed Autumn whispering to Twister. Summer followed their gaze and saw that from Twister's lips had emerged a tiny tornado, which Autumn gently blew toward Bluster's ankles. He tripped over it and gazed madly at his feet, searching for the invisible root or twig that tripped him. Autumn and Twister covered their giggles with their hands. Next to them, Quake offered his tea sandwich to Spring. She took a bite and exclaimed that he'd coated it in "just the right" amount of mustard seeds. Quake beamed with pride. Even Winter was enjoying the Weeds' company, bursting with laughter at one of Sleet's anecdotes. Thunderbolt refilled Summer's glass of lemonade and she took it with a smile, leaning back contentedly in her chair. It was summertime, her favorite season, and she had done what her season did best—grow something from nothing. In her case, a new friendship with Thunderbolt. And looking at her sisters and the Weeds, she thought, *Maybe a couple more friendships too.*

Elise Allen is the author of the young adult novel *Populazzi* and the chapter book *Anna's Icy Adventure*, based on Disney's *Frozen*. She cowrote the *New York Times* best-selling Elixir trilogy with Hilary Duff, and the Autumn Falls series with Bella Thorne. A longtime collaborator with the Jim Henson Company, she's written for *Sid the Science Kid* and *Dinosaur Train*.
www.eliseallen.com

Halle Stanford, an eight-time Emmy-nominated children's television producer, is in charge of creating children's entertainment at the Jim Henson Company. She currently serves as the executive producer on the award-winning series *Sid the Science Kid*, *Dinosaur Train*, *Pajanimals*, and *Doozers*.

Paige Pooler is an artist who loves to draw pictures for girls. You can find Paige's artwork in *American Girl* magazine and the Liberty Porter, Trading Faces, and My Sister the Vampire middle grade series.
www.paigepooler.com

The Jim Henson Company has remained an established leader in family entertainment for over fifty years and is the creator of such Emmy-nominated hits as *Sid the Science Kid*, *Dinosaur Train*, *Pajanimals*, and *Fraggle Rock*. The company is currently developing the Enchanted Sisters series as an animated TV property.
www.henson.com